Educating Arthur

A Quality Time™ Book

Library of Congress Cataloging-in-Publication Data

Graham, Amanda, 1961-
   Educating Arthur

   Sequel to: Who wants Arthur?
   Summary: Rambunctious adopted dog Arthur wreaks
havoc with his attempts to "help" the James family,
until they start training him with a rewards system.
   [1. Dogs--Training--Fiction] I. Gynell, Donna, ill.
II. Title.
PZ7.G751664Ed 1988 [E] 87-42756
ISBN 1-55532-436-3
ISBN 1-55532-411-8 (lib. bdg.)

North American edition first published in 1988 by

Gareth Stevens, Inc.
7317 West Green Tree Road
Milwaukee, WI 53223, USA

First published in Australia by Era Publications.
1 2 3 4 5 6 7 8 9 93 92 91 90 89 88

Educating Arthur

Story by Amanda Graham
Pictures by Donna Gynell

Gareth Stevens Publishing
Milwaukee

Arthur loved
chewing old slippers
for fun,
but today
there were more important
things to do.

Arthur had to help Melanie
fix her bike.

Melanie's mother needed Arthur's help potting plants.

Arthur had to help Grandpa
bake a cake.

Grandpa wasn't sure that Arthur
was really helping at all.

"Arthur wants to help," said Grandpa,
"so let's teach him how.
Every time he does something properly,
we will give him a reward."

Arthur learned
to put his slippers away
every time Melanie said "slippers."

"Slippers, Arthur."

Whenever he did it properly,
he was richly rewarded
with a hug and a dog biscuit.

Arthur learned to tidy his basket
every time Grandpa said "tidy."
"Tidy, Arthur."

Whenever he did it properly,
he was richly rewarded
with two hugs and two dog biscuits.

"Now," said Grandpa.
"Fetching the newspaper:
Fetch, Arthur."

It took quite some time
for Arthur to learn
to fetch the newspaper
in one piece.

MARTINA CRIES
AFTER MICK
WINS

AEROBICS INSTRUCTOR
SPLITS LEOTARD WHILE
EATING SALAD

23

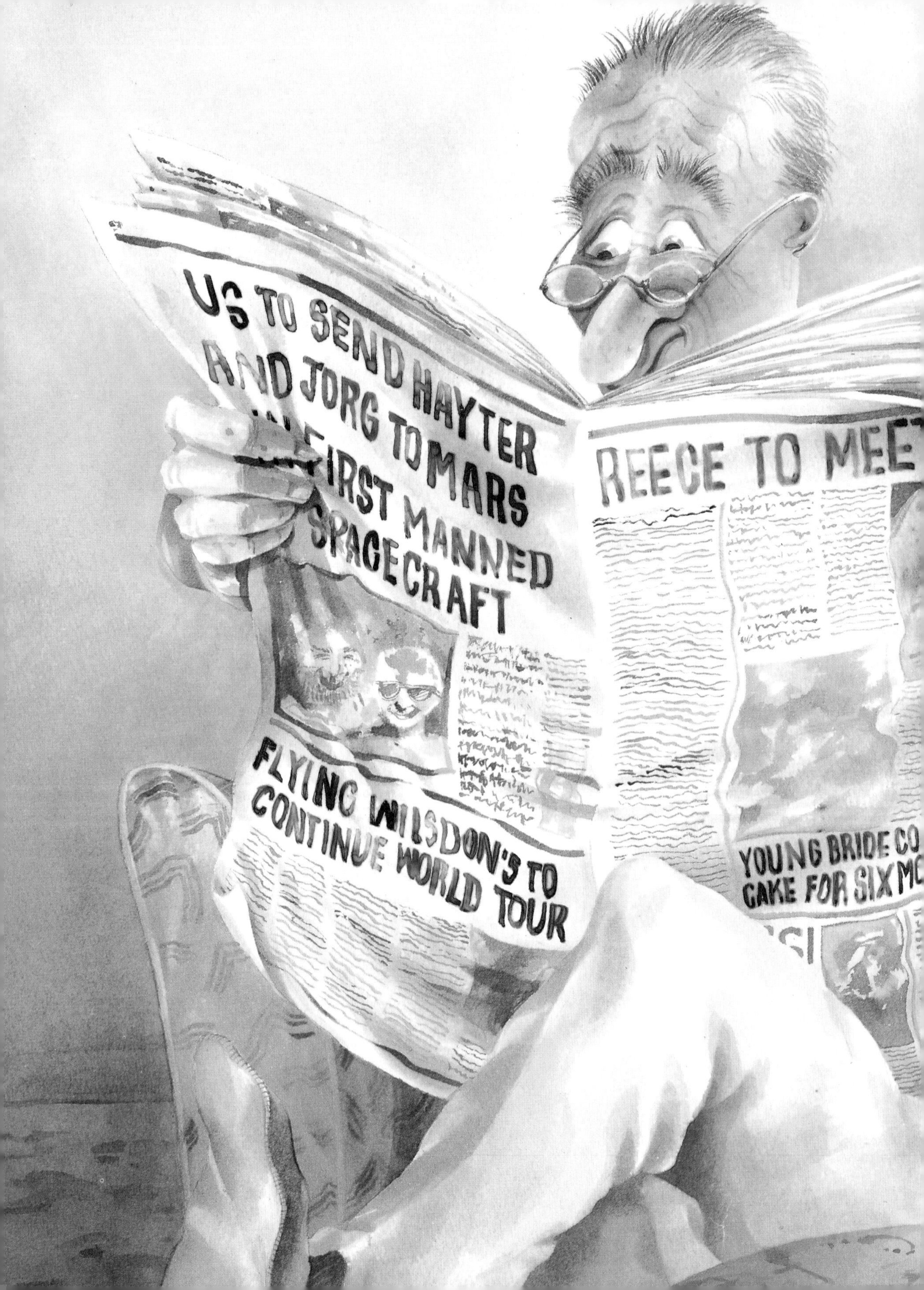
US TO SEND HAYTER
AND JORG TO MARS
FIRST MANNED
SPACECRAFT
FLYING WILSDON'S TO
CONTINUE WORLD TOUR
REECE TO MEE
YOUNG BRIDE CO
CAKE FOR SIX MO

But whenever
he did it properly,
he was richly rewarded
with three hugs
and three dog biscuits.

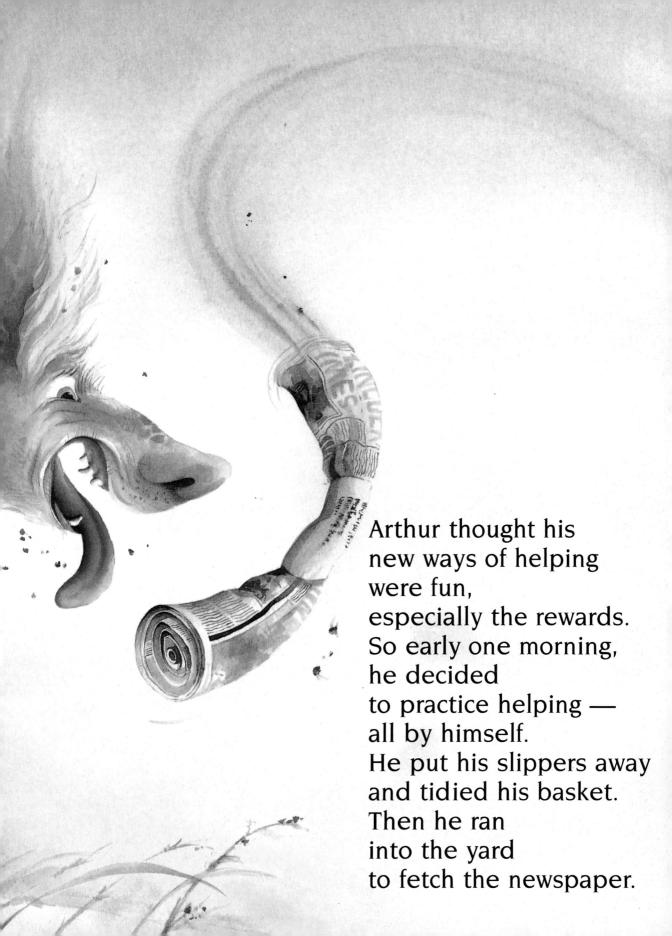

Arthur thought his
new ways of helping
were fun,
especially the rewards.
So early one morning,
he decided
to practice helping —
all by himself.
He put his slippers away
and tidied his basket.
Then he ran
into the yard
to fetch the newspaper.

Arthur went into Melanie's room
for his hugs and dog biscuits,
but she was asleep.

He went into Grandpa's room
for his hugs and dog biscuits,
but Grandpa was asleep, too.

So Arthur
collected his reward . . .

...all by himself!

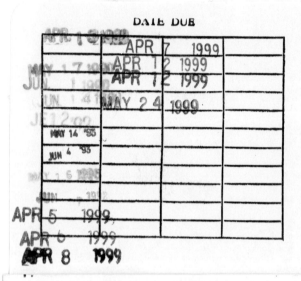

E
G

Graham, Amanda
Educating Arthur